ARES

God of War

BY TERI TEMPLE

ILLUSTRATED BY ROBERT SQUIER

Published by The Child's World®
1980 Lookout Drive • Mankato, MN 56003-1705
800-599-READ • www.childsworld.com

Acknowledgments
The Child's World®: Mary Berendes, Publishing Director
The Design Lab: Design and production
Red Line Editorial: Editorial direction

Design elements: Maksym Dragunov/Dreamstime;
Dreamstime

Photographs ©: Shutterstock Images, 5; Shutterstock
Images, 12; Andrey Burmakin/Shutterstock Images, 15;
Brigida Soriano/Shutterstock Images, 18; Bibi Saint-
Pol, 23; Shutterstock Images, 25; Titian, 26; Peter Paul
Rubens, 28

ISBN 9781614732556
LCCN 2012932426

Printed in the United States of America
Mankato, MN
July 2012
PA02119

CONTENTS

INTRODUCTION

ong ago in ancient Greece and Rome, most people believed that gods and goddesses ruled their world. Storytellers shared the adventures of these gods to help explain all the mysteries in life. The gods were immortal, meaning they lived forever. Their stories were full of love and tragedy, fearsome monsters, brave heroes, and struggles for power. The storytellers wove aspects of Greek customs and beliefs into the tales. Some stories told of the creation of the world and the origins of the gods. Others helped explain natural events such as earthquakes and storms. People believed the tales, which over time became myths.

The ancient Greeks and Romans worshiped the gods by building temples and statues in their honor. They felt the gods would protect and guide them. People passed down the myths through the generations by word of mouth. Later, famous poets such as Homer and Hesiod wrote them down. Today, these myths give us a unique look at what life was like in ancient Greece more than 2,000 years ago.

ANCIENT GREEK SOCIETIES

IN ANCIENT GREECE, CITIES, TOWNS, AND THEIR SURROUNDING FARMLANDS WERE CALLED CITY-STATES. THESE CITY-STATES EACH HAD THEIR OWN GOVERNMENTS. THEY MADE THEIR OWN LAWS. THE INDIVIDUAL CITY-STATES WERE VERY INDEPENDENT. THEY NEVER JOINED TO BECOME ONE WHOLE NATION. THEY DID, HOWEVER, SHARE A COMMON LANGUAGE, RELIGION, AND CULTURE.

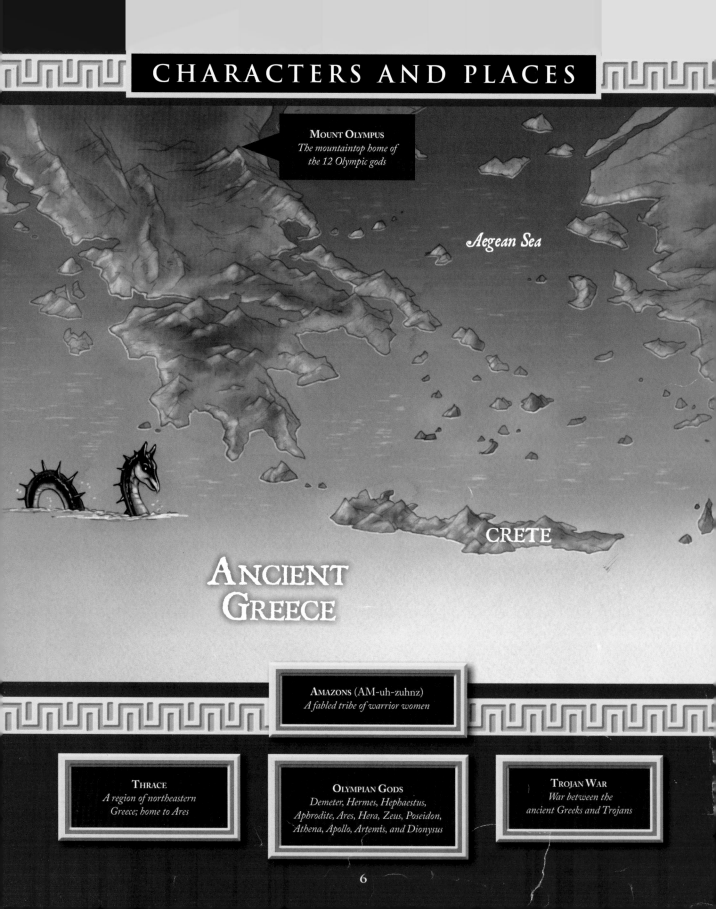

MOUNT OLYMPUS
*The mountaintop home of
the 12 Olympic gods*

Aegean Sea

CRETE

ANCIENT
GREECE

AMAZONS (AM-uh-zuhnz)
A fabled tribe of warrior women

THRACE
*A region of northeastern
Greece; home to Ares*

OLYMPIAN GODS
*Demeter, Hermes, Hephaestus,
Aphrodite, Ares, Hera, Zeus, Poseidon,
Athena, Apollo, Artemis, and Dionysus*

TROJAN WAR
*War between the
ancient Greeks and Trojans*

ALOADAE (al-oh-EY-dee)

Twin giants Otus and Ephialtes; sons of Poseidon

APHRODITE (af-roh-DY-tee)

Goddess of love and beauty; born of the sea foam; wife of Hephaestus; mother of Eros

ARES (AIR-eez)

God of war; son of Zeus and Hera; possible father of Eros

ATHENA (a-THEE-na)

Goddess of wisdom; daughter of Zeus

DEIMOS (DAHY-mos)

God of terror; son and attendant of Ares

ENYO (ih-NAHY-oh)

Goddess of war; companion of Ares

ERIS (EE-ris)

Goddess of strife; and attendant of Ares

HEPHAESTUS (huh-FES-tuhs)

God of fire and metalwork; son of Zeus and Hera; married to Aphrodite

HERA (HEER-uh)

Queen of the gods; married to Zeus

PHOBOS (FO-bos)

God of fear; son and attendant of Ares

ZEUS (ZOOS)

Supreme ruler of the heavens and weather and of the gods who lived on Mount Olympus; youngest son of Cronus and Rhea ; married to Hera; father of many gods and heroes

Hidden among the clouds atop Mount Olympus was a golden palace. It was the home of the Olympic gods. In the beginning there were only six. There were three brothers: Poseidon, Hades, and Zeus. The three sisters were Demeter, Hestia, and Hera. Together they ruled over the heavens and Earth. Zeus and Hera were their king and queen. Zeus had fought his father to gain control of the universe. The battle lasted for ten long years. Zeus eventually won, and peace settled over the land.

Zeus and Hera's marriage soon followed. It was a joyous celebration. Even nature celebrated by bursting into full bloom. When Hera discovered she was expecting their first child, the gods were thrilled. Zeus and Hera had high hopes for their child. As the child of the king and queen of the universe, their child would deserve the respect of gods and humans alike. All should have been perfect on Mount Olympus. However, nothing is ever perfect, even for the gods. The arrival of Ares was not at all what they expected.

As Ares grew, his skills and talents grew as well. He was very strong and swift and became the envy of his fellow gods. Despite his handsome face, Ares developed an extremely bad-tempered personality. Ares was self-centered and cruel. He seemed to care for nothing but battles and bloodshed. Ares got great pleasure out of causing pain and strife.

Being the god of war, Ares did not really care who won the fight. He just enjoyed the battles. Each day it was getting more difficult to govern the bloodthirsty god. Ares spread mostly hate and was becoming very hard to like. Even his parents grew to hate him. Most of the gods just chose to steer clear of Ares. All he seemed to do was stir up trouble.

Disappointed in their first son, Hera and Zeus went on to have three more children together. Their daughter Hebe was the gentle goddess of youth and cupbearer for the gods. She poured wine and was a delight to the gods following Ares. They named their other daughter Eileithyia. As the goddess of childbirth, Eileithyia was often seen helping her mother. Hera's final child was Hephaestus. He was a lame and ugly god of fire, but he was also kind. Ares never really got along with any of his siblings. Hephaestus would give Ares a great deal of grief.

Ancient Greeks considered Ares to be a manly man and a true warrior. He was mature, bearded, and dressed in full armor. He was tall, handsome, and always ready for battle. Ares wore a helmet and carried a sword, spear, and shield with pride.

Despite his good looks and battle skills, Ares was known to have a bad temper. He was also moody. At times Ares displayed a warrior's courage. Charging into combat with little caution, Ares often ended up injured. He would then have to leave the battlefield and return to Mount Olympus for treatment. Never one to mope, Ares would have his wounds tended and then jump right back into the battle. When the battle did not go his way, Ares was a sore loser. He often looked to the other gods for pity. He was always disappointed.

THRACE

ARES'S TEMPER MADE HIM UNWELCOME IN THE PALACE ON MOUNT OLYMPUS. SO ARES SPENT MUCH OF HIS TIME IN THRACE. THRACE WAS A LARGE REGION IN THE BALKAN PENINSULA. THE BALKAN PENINSULA WAS LOCATED IN THE SOUTHEASTERN PART OF EUROPE. IT WAS SURROUNDED ON THREE SIDES BY WATER. THE ANCIENT THRACIANS WERE A VIOLENT PEOPLE. THEY

Ares traveled a great deal, seeking out and starting wars. His decorated chariot and fire-breathing stallions made a big impression when he rode into battle. The four horses were named Flame, Red-Fire, Tumult, and Fear. Enyo, a goddess of war, drove the chariot. She held a torch up to light the way for Ares's many followers.

His closest companions were two of his sons. Phobos was the god of terror. Deimos was the god of fear. Together they helped their father create chaos and confusion on the fields of war. Another loyal follower was Eris. The goddess of strife owned a magical golden apple. When she threw it among enemies it caused wars to break out. Along with Enyo, they stirred up fear in the hearts of warriors.

MARATHON

IN 490 BC A GREAT BATTLE WAS FOUGHT IN MARATHON, GREECE. A SMALL ATHENIAN ARMY DEFEATED A MUCH LARGER PERSIAN FORCE. LEGEND STATES THAT A YOUNG GREEK MAN RAN BACK TO ATHENS TO DECLARE THE VICTORY. MARATHON WAS 26.2 MILES (42.2 KM) FROM ATHENS. PHEIDIPPIDES RAN THE ENTIRE DISTANCE WITHOUT STOPPING. THE MARATHON THAT ATHLETES RUN

Ares gleefully waved his sword when he heard the sounds of fighting. The spirit Discord would lead the way. Panic, Pain, Famine, and Anger were just some of the vicious spirits that followed in Ares's wake. They gladly followed Ares off to war.

Ares felt most at home on the battlefield. He rarely sought revenge against individuals. He saved up all his anger for the larger military conflicts. It was during these battles that Ares used his weapons with deadly accuracy. He laughed at the misery of others.

Ares was not the only god of war though. Athena was also a goddess of war and Ares's biggest rival. Together they represented the two sides of war. Ares preferred to fight using brute force and muscle. He would rather use a weapon than his brains. Athena represented the intellectual side of war. She preferred battle strategy to mindless killing. Athena viewed war as an unfortunate but necessary evil. Ancient Greeks much preferred Athena's methods.

Athena often looked for ways to humble her half-brother. She could easily outsmart him on the battlefield. This made Ares furious. Just seeing Athena sent him into a wild rage. The rivalry of these two siblings came to a head during the great Trojan War.

The Trojan War was an epic battle fought between the ancient Greeks and the citizens of the city of Troy. It began over the kidnapping of the Greek queen Helen. Aphrodite, the goddess of love and beauty, helped the Trojan prince Paris kidnap Helen. The goddess also convinced Ares to side with her and the Trojans. Ares could never resist Aphrodite's charms. Since Ares had no loyalty to either side, he readily agreed.

It seemed all the gods on Olympus had an interest in this war. Ares joined Aphrodite, Apollo, and Artemis in aiding the people of Troy. Athena, Hera, Poseidon, Hermes, and Hephaestus sided with Greece. They all had grudges against the Trojans.

During the heat of battle, Ares found himself fighting the Greek hero Diomedes. He was also Ares's son! Athena came to Diomedes's aid. In doing so she gravely injured Ares with her spear. Ares's howls of pain were as

WARFARE IN ANCIENT GREECE

WARFARE WAS COMMON IN ANCIENT GREECE. CITY-STATES WERE ALWAYS FIGHTING. THEY FOUGHT EACH OTHER OVER LAND BOUNDARIES. THEY FOUGHT TOGETHER TO DEFEND AGAINST

loud as that of 9,000 men. Aphrodite rushed to his side only to be wounded herself. Eventually they both made it back to Mount Olympus. Zeus was disgusted with his son. The Trojan War ended without the help of Ares.

INVADERS. SOMETIMES THEY EVEN FOUGHT AS INVADERS. THEY RAIDED OTHER COUNTRIES FOR THEIR RICHES. GREEK SOLDIERS, CALLED HOPLITES, FOUGHT IN A SPECIAL FORMATION. SOLDIERS STOOD IN A LINE SHOULDER TO SHOULDER. THIS LINE WAS CALLED A *PHALANX*. IT ALLOWED EACH SOLDIER TO PROTECT HIS NEIGHBOR WITH HIS SHIELD. SOLDIERS ALSO USED HELMETS, SHIELDS, AND SWORDS.

Ares would have many affairs, but only one true love. It was the goddess Aphrodite. For Ares it was love at first sight. Ares had an opportunity to marry Aphrodite. But his brother Hephaestus ruined his chances. His mother Hera had treated Hephaestus cruelly. As a master craftsman he used all his skills to create a beautiful golden throne. Hephaestus gave it to Hera as a gift. Unable to resist, Hera accepted the magnificent throne. But as soon as Hera sat on the throne she was trapped. None of the other gods could figure out how to release her. When they asked Hephaestus to free Hera, he refused. When Dionysus, the god of wine, got Hephaestus drunk, he agreed to reveal the throne's secret. Hephaestus drove a hard bargain though. He would only release Hera if she promised him Aphrodite as his wife. The deal was sealed and the two were married.

This did not stop Ares. Aphrodite did not like the lame and ugly Hephaestus. She much preferred his more handsome brother Ares. Aphrodite and Ares decided to meet in secret. They thought they could outsmart the god of fire. But Hephaestus was no fool. He learned of their meetings and set a trap to catch them. Hephaestus used his skill as a master craftsman to create a magical net. Made of the finest bronze links, it was invisible to the eye. One day Hephaestus found Aphrodite and Ares asleep.

Hephaestus cast his net over and trapped them. Hephaestus hoped to embarrass Ares into no longer seeing Aphrodite. When the two awoke, all the gods and goddesses were waiting to pass judgment. Sadly Hephaestus learned that the other gods could not blame Ares because Aphrodite was so beautiful. No one could resist her charms. Ares had managed to outsmart his brother Hephaestus after all.

It was true that Aphrodite was the one true love of Ares. She was by no means the only love, however. Ares caught the eye of many maidens despite his unpleasant nature. Ares would never marry though. Yet his love affairs produced many children. Many of these children inherited their father's warlike personality or were connected with war.

There was his son the Greek hero Diomedes. Then there was the serpent Drakon, who guarded his father Ares's sacred spring. His children with Aphrodite were the most famous. Together they had three sons and one daughter. Their sons Phobos and Deimos were Ares's constant companions on any battlefield. Their daughter Harmonia was the complete opposite of Ares. She grew up to be the lovely goddess of harmony. Aphrodite and Ares's youngest son was Eros, the mischievous god of love.

CADMUS AND HARMONIA

CADMUS WAS THE FOUNDER OF THE GREEK CITY OF THEBES. HIS WIFE HARMONIA WAS THE BEAUTIFUL DAUGHTER OF APHRODITE AND ARES. WHILE BUILDING THEBES, ALL OF CADMUS'S COMPANIONS WERE KILLED BY DRAKON. THE GIANT SERPENT WAS GUARDING A SACRED SPRING. IN A FIT OF RAGE, CADMUS KILLED DRAKON WITH A STONE. AS PUNISHMENT ARES CHANGED CADMUS INTO A SERPENT. HEARTBROKEN, HARMONIA

Ares was also the father of two of the Amazons' most famous queens—Queen Penthesilea and Queen Hippolyte. The Amazons were a race of warrior women. They lived in a remote region of Asia. Barbaric and fierce, the Amazons worshiped Ares as the father of their tribe. Yet men were not allowed to be part of their families. Ares had a special connection to the Amazons. He supported the Amazons and their wars.

Queen Penthesilea aided the Trojans with her father in the Trojan War. Ares had given Penthesilea a fabulous set of armor. She used it to kill many of the Greek warriors. The mighty Greek hero Achilles finally brought her down.

Queen Hippolyte was the other Amazon daughter of Ares. Ares gave Hippolyte his war belt. To him it symbolized her warrior spirit. The hero Heracles was sent to fetch Hippolyte's magical belt as one of his 12 labors. Hippolyte was killed as the Amazons defended her. Many of the children of Ares became casualties of the very thing their father loved—war.

PLANETS AND THE GODS

ANCIENT GREEKS BELIEVED THERE WAS A CONNECTION BETWEEN THE PLANETS AND MYTHOLOGY. THE PLANETS IN OUR SOLAR SYSTEM REPRESENTED THEIR VARIOUS GODS. WE CALL THE PLANETS BY THE NAMES THE ANCIENT ROMANS GAVE THEM. SATURN WAS CRONUS, THE ORIGINAL TITAN. GAEA WAS MOTHER EARTH AND HER HUSBAND WAS URANUS. THE THREE BROTHERS WERE JUPITER,

NEPTUNE, AND PLUTO FOR ZEUS, POSEIDON, AND HADES. MERCURY REPRESENTED HERMES AND VENUS WAS APHRODITE. MARS WAS THE RED PLANET. IT STOOD FOR ARES. THE RED COLOR WAS A SYMBOL OF WAR AND BLOOD TO

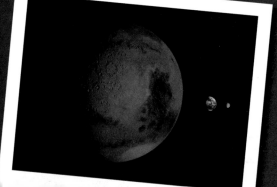

Ares rarely spent time off of the battlefield, but he was once forced to stay away. The Aloadae giants kept Ares from battle for 13 months. These two brothers, Otus and Ephialtes, were so strong even the gods could not hurt them. The giants believed they were great enough to take over Mount Olympus. Ares tried to stop them but was defeated. The giants chained Ares in bonds too strong for him to break. Then Otus and Ephialtes sealed Ares in a bronze jar.

Ares struggled to free himself for 13 months. When Ares became too weak, the giants' stepmother began to feel pity for him. She sent a message to Hermes, the messenger god. Hermes was the swiftest of all the gods. So he snuck in and stole Ares without Otus and Ephialtes knowing. Hermes helped Ares return to Mount Olympus. Ares spent many days in the palace, recovering from his months in the jar. It was a humiliating and humbling experience for the mighty god of war.

SISYPHUS

SISYPHUS WAS A CLEVER HUMAN WHO TRIED TO CHEAT DEATH. THE GOD OF DEATH CAME FOR SISYPHUS WHEN IT WAS HIS TIME TO DIE. INSTEAD SISYPHUS TRICKED DEATH, WHO BECAME CHAINED TO A CHAIR. AS LONG

Ares was mainly worshiped in Sparta and Thrace. His worshipers prayed to him for courage and victory in battle. Yet few people wanted to actually start a war. To them all Ares caused was mayhem and destruction. Therefore his temples were rarely visited.

Ancient Romans had a god equal to Ares. It was their god of war named Mars. Mars was a much more popular god. Early on, Mars was known as the spirit of spring and fertility. Mars was also the father of Romulus and Remus, the founders of Rome. Several festivals were held in his honor. These festivals all involved cleansing and purifying rituals. Mars became the god of war after the Romans invaded Greece. They adopted much of the Greek culture including the stories surrounding the Greek gods.

Ares may have been the least-liked god on Mount Olympus. Still, he left his own unique mark on the myths and stories passed down through the ages.

PRINCIPAL GODS OF GREEK MYTHOLOGY –
A FAMILY TREE

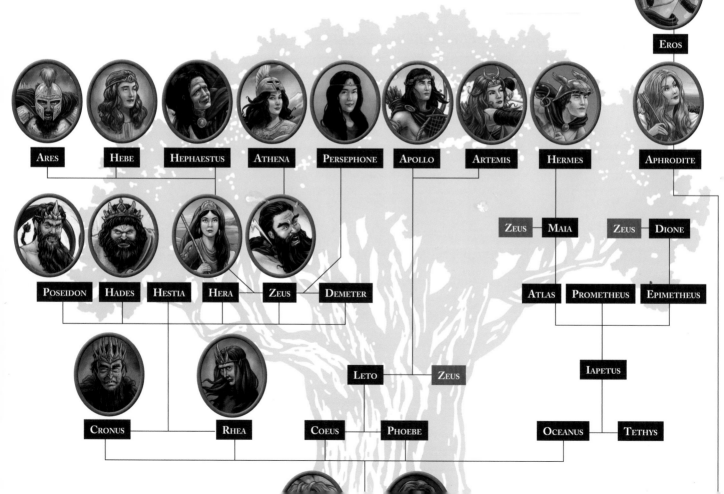

ARES | HEBE | HEPHAESTUS | ATHENA | PERSEPHONE | APOLLO | ARTEMIS | HERMES | EROS | APHRODITE

ZEUS — MAIA | ZEUS — DIONE

POSEIDON | HADES | HESTIA | HERA | ZEUS | DEMETER | ATLAS | PROMETHEUS | EPIMETHEUS

IAPETUS

LETO | ZEUS

CRONUS | RHEA | COEUS | PHOEBE | OCEANUS | TETHYS

THE ROMAN GODS

As the Roman Empire expanded by conquering new lands the Romans often took on aspects of the customs and beliefs of the people they conquered. From the ancient Greeks they took their arts and sciences. They also adopted many of their gods and the myths that went with them into their religious beliefs. While the names were changed, the stories and legends found a new home.

ZEUS: *Jupiter*
King of the Gods, God of Sky and Storms
Symbols: *Eagle and Thunderbolt*

HERA: *Juno*
Queen of the Gods, Goddess of Marriage
Symbols: *Peacock, Cow, and Crow*

POSEIDON: *Neptune*
God of the Sea and Earthquakes
Symbols: *Trident, Horse, and Dolphin*

HADES: *Pluto*
God of the Underworld
Symbols: *Helmet, Metals, and Jewels*

ATHENA: *Minerva*
Goddess of Wisdom, War, and Crafts
Symbols: *Owl, Shield, and Olive Branch*

ARES: *Mars*
God of War
Symbols: *Vulture and Dog*

ARTEMIS: *Diana*
Goddess of Hunting and Protector of Animals
Symbols: *Stag and Moon*

APOLLO: *Apollo*
God of the Sun, Healing, Music, and Poetry
Symbols: *Laurel, Lyre, Bow, and Raven*

HEPHAESTUS: *Vulcan*
God of Fire, Metalwork, and Building
Symbols: *Fire, Hammer, and Donkey*

APHRODITE: *Venus*
Goddess of Love and Beauty
Symbols: *Dove, Sparrow, Swan, and Myrtle*

EROS: *Cupid*
God of Love
Symbols: *Quiver and Arrows*

HERMES: *Mercury*
God of Travels and Trade
Symbols: *Staff, Winged Sandals, and Helmet*

FURTHER INFORMATION

BOOKS

Green, Jen. *Ancient Greek Myths*. New York: Gareth Stevens, 2010.

Napoli, Donna Jo. *Treasury of Greek Mythology: Classic Stories of Gods, Goddesses, Heroes & Monsters*. Washington, DC: National Geographic Society, 2011.

Smith, Charles R. Jr. *The Mighty 12: Superheroes of Greek Myth*. New York: Little, Brown, 2008.

WEB SITES

Visit our Web site for links about Ares:
childsworld.com/links

Note to Parents, Teachers, and Librarians: We routinely verify our Web links to make sure they are safe and active sites. So encourage your readers to check them out!

INDEX